PREP
2/18

A FRIEND IS SOMEONE WHO LIKES YOU

joan walsh anglund

Houghton Mifflin Harcourt
Boston   New York

With all my love,
for my twin great-granddaughters,
Rose and Peach,
the next generation.

www.hmhco.com

The text type was set in Perpetua.

ISBN: 978-0-544-99919-0

Manufactured in China
SCP 10 9 8 7 6 5 4 3 2 1
4500673599

A friend is someone who likes you.

It can be a boy . . .

It can be a girl . . .

or a cat . . .

or a dog . . .

or even a white mouse.

A tree can be a different kind of friend.
It doesn't talk to you, but you know it
likes you, because it gives you apples . . .
or pears . . . or cherries . . . or,
sometimes, a place to swing.

A brook can be a friend in a special way. It talks to you with splashy gurgles. It cools your toes and lets you sit quietly beside it when you don't feel like speaking.

The wind can be a friend too.
It sings soft songs to you at night
when you are sleepy and feeling lonely.
Sometimes it calls to you to play. It
pushes you from behind as you walk
and makes the leaves dance for you. It
is always with you wherever you go,
and that's how you know it likes you.

Sometimes you don't know who your friends are. Sometimes they are there all the time, but you walk right past them and don't notice that they like you in a special way.

And then you think you don't have any friends.

Then you must stop hurrying and rushing so fast . . .

and move very slowly, and look
around carefully, to see someone
who smiles at you in a special way . . .
or a dog that wags its tail extra
hard whenever you are near . . .
or a tree that lets you climb it easily . . .
or a brook that lets you be
quiet when you want to be quiet.
Sometimes you have to find your friend.

Some people have lots and lots of friends . . .

and some people have quite a few friends . . .

but everyone . . .
everyone in the whole world has at least one friend.

Where did you find yours?

I had always dreamed of writing and illustrating children's books. When I first met my husband, Bob, I shared my dream with him. At the time, I was working in advertising doing artwork for Marshall Field and Company in Chicago.

Some years later, we lived happily in Evanston, Illinois, married with our two children, Joy and Todd. After several years, Bob's work necessitated our moving to New York City. It was hard for my children to say goodbye to their dear friends and their cousins in the countryside.

In New York, I felt very alone, and my children struggled to make friends. I felt isolated, and I was homesick.

Out of these lonely feelings came *A Friend Is Someone Who Likes You*. I wrote the words in my little green steno pad. When Bob came home from work, he found my pad and liked my writing. He asked me how I would illustrate what I had written. Remembering rural Illinois, I drew my daughter and son under a tree. I drew pictures of a little brook and climbing trees and many more illustrations based on our experiences with my sister and her children.

One day, I received a phone call. The voice said: "This is Margaret McElderry, an editor at Harcourt Brace. We would like to publish your book." I asked, "My book?" She answered, "Yes, *A Friend Is Someone Who Likes You.*" Bob had taken the book to several publishers and helped make my dream of writing and illustrating children's books come true.

This act of kindness and love changed my whole life.

Now, sixty years after its first publication, I hope you share these words and pictures with someone very special and dear to you.

Joan Walsh Anglund